I wish

Christoph Niemann

GREENWILLOW BOOKS

An Imprint of HarperCollinsPublishers

I wish

Copyright © 2022 by Christoph Niemann
All rights reserved. Manufactured in Italy.
For information address HarperCollins Children's Books,
a division of HarperCollins Publishers,
195 Broadway, New York, NY 10007.
www.harpercollinschildrens.com

The images were drawn digitally in Adobe Photoshop.

Library of Congress Cataloging-in-Publication Data

Names: Niemann, Christoph, author, illustrator.
Title: I wish / Christoph Niemann.
Description: First edition. | New York, NY : Greenwillow Books,
an Imprint of HarperCollins Publishers, [2022] | Audience: Ages 4–8. |
Audience: Grades K–1. |
Summary: In this wordless picture book, a young girl finds
a wrapped gift and wonders what might be inside.
Identifiers: LCCN 2022008188 | ISBN 9780063219793 (hardcover)
Subjects: CYAC: Stories without words. | Imagination—Fiction. |
LCGFT: Wordless picture books.
Classification: LCC PZ7.N56848 Iaw 2022 | DDC [E]—dc23
LC record available at https://lccn.loc.gov/2022008188

22 23 24 25 26 RTLO 10 9 8 7 6 5 4 3 2 1
First Edition

GREENWILLOW BOOKS

for Arthur

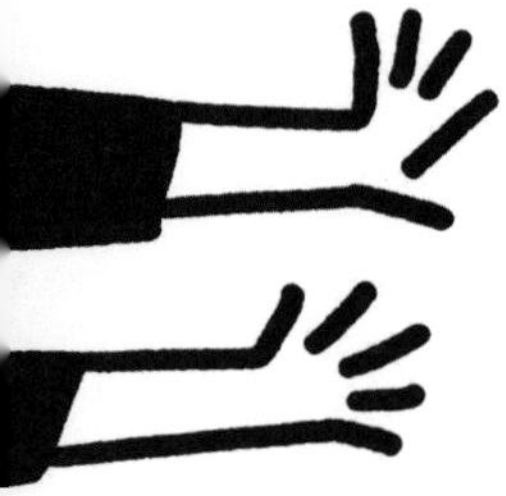

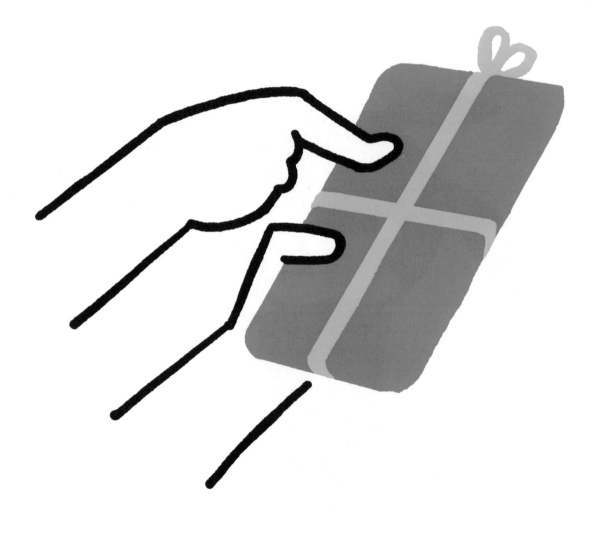

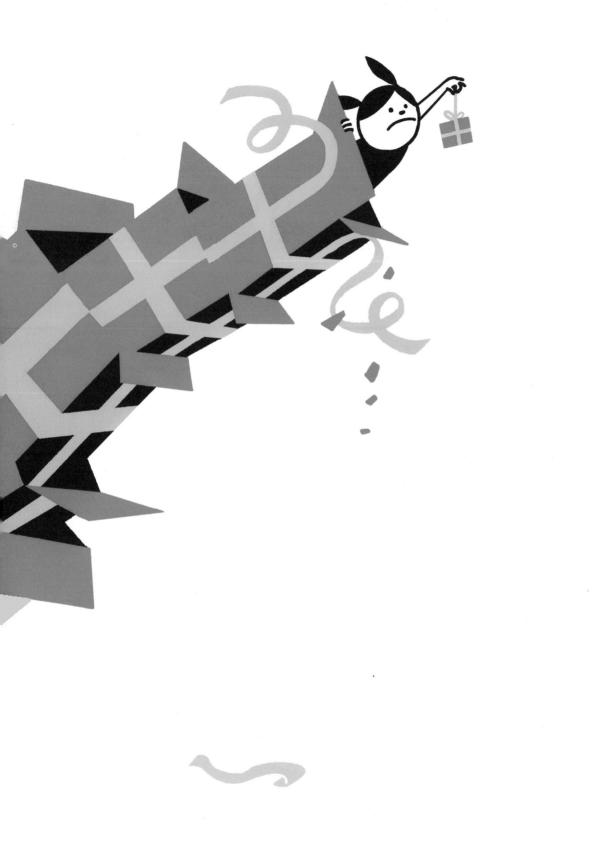

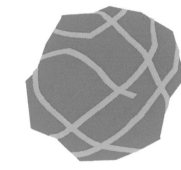

the

end